GOOD NIGHT, GOOD NIGHT

Written and illustrated by

HELEN H. WU

Good Night, Good Night
Written and illustrated by Helen H. Wu
Editor: Angeline Oppenheimer
www.helenhwu.com

TO MY LITTLE GEORGE

Stars twinkle,
The bright moon rises.
An owl hoots,
Piercing the silence.
Good night, good night,
It's time to sleep tight.

The little monkey,
Wide awake.

"Why don't you sleep?"
Asks the snake.

"I'm not ready,
For I'm hungry."

Hush my little baby,
Your supper is coming.

Hush my little baby,
Close your eyes,
And sleep till morning.

The Little monkey wriggles.

"What's the matter?"
Asks the jackal.

"I don't want to be fussy.
But something is wrong with my tummy."

Hush my little baby,

Your tummy needs some rubbing.

Hush my little baby,

Close your eyes,

And sleep till morning.

The little monkey whines.

"What could be wrong?"
Asks the porcupine.

"My pants are wet,
Could it be my sweat?"

Hush my little baby,

A dry pair of pants is waiting.

Hush my little baby,

Close your eyes,

And sleep till morning.

The little monkey looks around.

"What are you waiting for?"
Asks the greyhound.

"I need a bedtime story,
Full of dwarves and fairies."

Hush my little baby,

A tale you'll soon be hearing.

Hush my little baby,

Close your eyes,

And sleep till morning.

The little monkey yawns.

I'm ready to sleep to dawn.

For first, mama dear,

There is something you need to hear.

Hush my little baby,

My ears are ready and waiting.

Hush my little baby,

Close your eyes,

And sleep till morning.

Mama dear, I love you.
It will always be true.
To the moon and back,
My love will never slack.

I love you too, little munchkin.
Day will soon be coming.
Good night, good night,
Sleep tight till the morning light.

More Books by Helen H. Wu

www.helenhwu.com

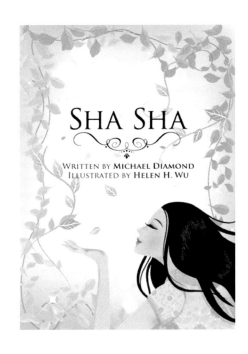

Made in the USA
Lexington, KY
07 June 2019